AVIAN

NEEL MUKHERJEE

Avian

CENTER FOR WRITERS & TRANSLATORS
THE AMERICAN UNIVERSITY OF PARIS

—

SYLPH EDITIONS

For Mimi and Milou, and Christopher (of course)

I

She will forget the name of the book she read as a child and how it ended, but she will understand, much later, that the story has stayed as a kind of haunting.

II

It begins like this. In an island far, far away on an unnamed sea, there live only children, who sleep for most of their days and nights, and have rich, full dreams, dreams more real to them than the embodied, tangible world of sand and sea and trees and birds of all hues flitting through and around and above them. The children have no language except one in their dreams which they use to communicate with each other. It does everything that a language is supposed to do: expresses wishes, feelings, states of mind, desires. It is the medium through which they tell each other stories, and things that have no discernible purpose except to bind them together as a community, as friends; a surplus, then, over and above the functional use. But they have no language in their waking state, which, in any case, does not form a major segment of their day. When they wake up they have no recollection of the language they used in their dreams, or, more accurately, they don't feel the need to remember it since all the uses that a language serves have been fulfilled while they were asleep.

Then a stranger arrives, no one knows from where. He is a man of indeterminate age, the only grown-up on the island. He may even have a monkey perched on his shoulder and something that she learns later is a fool's cap on his head. No one knows why or how he has fetched up in this remote place, but he readily makes friends with all the children and then, gradually, starts to appear in their dreams. A strange thing begins to happen: slowly, the children's dreams start to die out. First, the colours fade. Then the chattering is reduced to a murmur, the words become fewer and fewer, with great straits of silence separating them, until the tiny, scattered archipelago of words disappears entirely. A general thinning happens concurrently: all that density of other children, of birds and animals and rocks and stones and trees, begins to diminish, until the desolate dreams begin to resemble a just-begun pencil drawing on a blank page. Then the page turns white.

She remembers the drawing on this page of the book: there's no drawing; it's a blank page.

In the white blankness of the children's dreams, the stranger appears – a giant now, in the absence of anything else to give him scale and perspective – to tell them that he has made musical instruments out of their dreams. To retrieve them, the children will have to buy these instruments and learn how to play them.

Sure enough, next day, during their waking hours, the children find the stranger on the sandy shore of a cove, with scores of musical instruments spread out in front of him, zithers, lutes, recorders, clarinets, virginals, oboes, flutes, harps, horns, trumpets, bassoons, saxophones, lyres…At first the children think that it's the profusion that confuses them, then they realize that it stems from their inability to communicate with each other – the man has stolen their dream language.

Helter-skelter they run. They are like ants on a white page with a margin of blues – shading, in overlapping, gently curving, crinkled bands, from light to dark – for the sea. The man lifts his head and laughs. His mouth is a black cave; red tendrils and spatters issue from it and spill across the crevasse of the binding in the middle to the next page.

Some of the braver children start the long and arduous process of reclaiming their dreams. A shock awaits them. No one can tell whose dreams have gone into making which instrument, so the children choose blindly, only to discover that the matching of instrument to buyer is all wrong. Each child's dream begins with confusion, which mounts and mounts until the experience of dreaming, so far life-giving, becomes debilitating, a movement into nightmare, reducing the children to blank, hollow-eyed, miserable creatures. They roam the island, singly, like spectres, deprived of animation and energy.

And the man who has brought all this about? Her impression – unreliable, she'll be the first to admit – is that he either doesn't know or is not telling which instrument corresponds to which child. But he is in for a surprise too: watching their friends turn into automata after learning to play the instruments they bought, the remaining children are discouraged from buying. The fear is that the stranger has wrought some malignant magic through his wares and turned their friends into the living dead. So all the profiteering genius of the man comes to nothing. She imagines a variation on the earlier two-page spread here: this time, the strew is of harps and pianos and guitars and flutes. Straddling the cleft in the middle is a spread of unsold musical instruments – here, the middle strings of a harp fall into the dip as the rest of it bends out over the other side; there, a piano has two legs on the left-hand page, one almost disappearing into the binding, and the last one barely making it over the lip to the right-hand page – while the man, his mouth firmly shut, looks down on the waste with a face that is at once puzzled, angry, defeated.

She has no memory of how the story ends. Or, put another way, she cannot imagine it.

III

When they're not trying not to look at her, she catches them, by accident, looking at her, embarrassed and baffled, maybe even a touch fearful.

There was the evening when her son and daughter, five and three respectively, were entertained by their mother's mimicry of bird calls at dinner, the boy asking questions, 'Mummy, is that a blue jay? Is that a tit?', both of them imitating some of her cries, finding it such a jape that mummy was replying to their questions in birdsong; until it slowly dawned on them that mummy had not given them saucers of grain as part of an elaborate game that was going to end soon, the saucers whisked away with peals of laughter and plates of pasta with cheese or fried eggs conjured to replace them. Even when she was showing them how to peck at the grains, and the children were imitating her, all of them down on the kitchen lino on their hands and knees, heads bobbing furiously at a small saucer of uncooked split red lentils, at some point the playacting began to congeal in the children's minds into something else – something less playful, something that had crossed a boundary between safe and unsafe, between

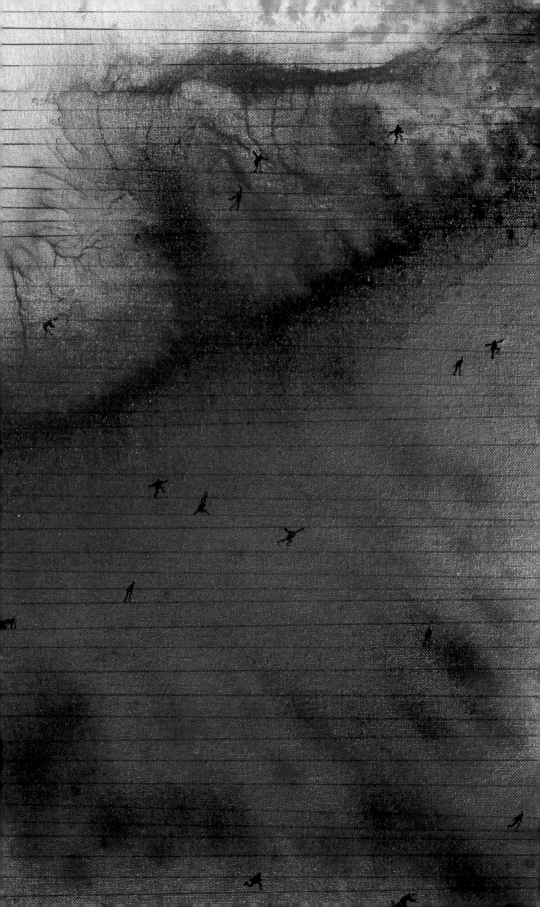

the admissible and the forbidden. They couldn't have put it into words; it was just an inchoate feeling, brushed by terror.

It was the arrival of their father, coming to pick them up to stay with him for the weekend, that unfroze the children as if a wand had been waved to remove a spell. They ran to him, clutched his legs, and burst into tears.

'Krrri-krrri-*weeeee*-krrri, krrri-krrri-*weeeee*-krrri, krrri-krrri-*weeeee*-krrri,' she sang with focused intent.

The research grant proposal had begun with the risky gambit of a childhood anecdote. It went like this: 'Which child has not grown up with stories, or at least childhood observations, that have gone on to have outsized effects on her or his adult life? As a small child, Barbara McClintock noticed a sparse, random scatter of red and purple-black grains on an otherwise uniformly creamy golden-yellow corncob. When she asked why, someone extemporized a story about how they were the corn's eyes; God had placed them in these sentinel cobs, which only grew along the perimeter of the fields, where they could watch over the family they enclosed. Who can say whether a fascination with that story did not result in her pathbreaking work on genetic transposition? The perfumer Bertrand Duchaufour tells the story of how his earliest childhood memory is of the smell of incense and burning wood. Is it entirely fanciful to see a strong, legible line between that memory and Duchaufour's greatest contribution to fragrances in bringing a delectable smokiness to the heart of most of the perfumes that he has designed?

'A similar "myth of origin" of my intellectual endeavour could be seen to lie in a trope that kept recurring in some fairy tales I read as a child. Someone loses his way in a forest and has to shelter under a tree at night. As he is falling asleep, he hears a bird-couple in their nest in the branches above talk in a language that he can understand. Mr and Mrs Bird are discussing his fate – the choices that face him, the tricky situation he finds himself in, the solution to the problem, what he needs to do. In the morning he gets up, acts on the advice of the bird-couple despite its seemingly counterintuitive and frankly impossible nature or its enormous costliness, and finds his way out of crisis.

'What was innocent magic in childhood morphed into
a different kind of magic as I grew up: intellectual curiosity,
specifically, to investigate the nature of bird songs and avian
communication. This project on the intersecting area of birdsong
and human speech, particularly in its focus on both vocal learning
and perceptual learning, aims to bring together computational
neuroscience, philosophy of language, developmental biology, and
cognitive psychology...'

She was advised against the use of the word 'delectable', the
illustrative use of a perfumer in a science grant application, the
inclusion of autobiographical elements, the subjective language,
and, above all, the bringing in of philosophy of language, all of
which she ignored because she had what she called 'a gut feeling'.
Years of training in science had not managed to wash out of her
either the belief in or the frequent use of the words 'a gut feeling',
nor had it persuaded her to dress them up as the more acceptable
'intuition'.

The project was offered the biggest grant in the history of
her institution.

For as long as she has lived in this house, she has looked at this
view from her third-floor bedroom window: the upper half of
a huge lime-blossom tree in the garden below, in the summer a
green tower, that elusive fragrance flitting in and out of her open
window in May so maddening that she sometimes had to shut her
window in the middle of the night – beauty could be a maddening
thing – and in the winter a cathedral of ribs and bones. It was
the season closest to her heart and mind because it was during
this time that she could see, unhindered by the green growth of
summer, all the bird life that used the tree for its various purposes.
If one discounted the ugly hulking jackdaws, the commonest used
to be magpies, with their cries that brought to mind the scraping
of the bottom of a harsh metal vessel with something harsher,
great tits and blue tits, robins, blackbirds (oh, their songs!),
chaffinches (those rapid-fire Morse dots of the beginning of their
song, ending in a short flourish of wavy dashes), wood pigeons.
'Used to be' because, although they're fairly abundant now, they
have been surpassed, both numerically and auditorily, by vast feral
populations of rose-ringed parakeets. There are several stories to

explain the presence of this exotic tropical species in a cold, wet, grey, inhospitable northern city – escapees from a film set that adapted to the climate then bred, or from the enclosed tropical section of a botanical garden – but she's not sure whether these aren't urban myths. Whatever the origin of their appearance, the magic of a shrieking dazzle of the brightest green flitting against the grimy sky and alighting, cooing and clicking their tongues and making guttural whirrs on trees by the dozen, never tarnishes for her. She has vague memories of a novel in which an urban domestic garden in her own city fills up with rare and flamboyant tropical birds, some even extinct – and here is the real version, life imitating fiction.

Once, she is gifted with the sight of a male great spotted woodpecker (not a rare bird, not in the slightest), with the surprising flash of his red bottom and red crown, clinging vertically on to the trunk instead of perching on a branch, unaware of her of course but as if playing hide and seek, twirling around on the trunk, so that he is hidden behind its girth one moment, then peeking out again and reappearing on the side visible to her. Finches and tits like quivering punctuation marks, alive with movement and song. There will be a single one, sitting on a branch, singing, then another will fly in and sit on another branch, as if neither has seen or heard the other. Sometimes they will sit in a random distribution – a pair on one branch, a single one on another, three or four on yet another, then another solitary one... Is it her mind that knits them into a community or are they really one, reading sounds and movements and other sense data that are opaque to her?

Walking out of her house one morning in the snow on her way to the supermarket, she becomes conscious of the earworm going through her head, and struggles briefly to identify it. When she does, she laughs at the absurdity – it's 'Ice, ice, baby, ice, ice', a rap song from the late 1980s. What on earth? How, from where? And then she pays attention to the repeated sound surfacing over the background noise then disappearing, surfacing, disappearing, surfacing, disappearing... or rather, it's not she paying attention but the sound picking her out and insisting that she notice. It's a two-note bird call. Ice-ice, ice-ice, ice-ice...

Dusk, another day. In the darkening blue light a blackbird composes variations. Who is he waiting for at this hour? Who will hear him but humans? The thought distracts her. She forgets to feed the children, the pasta water boils over and the saucepan runs dry and starts to burn. The smoke alarm goes off. She's distracted even while opening the kitchen window, waving a tea towel at the ceiling near the alarm. Why is the bird still singing? Each phrase, each line is different in a few notes; no other word for it but *variations*.

IV

Here's an event over which she has perfect recall. She is twenty, in the penultimate year of her neuroscience doctorate. She goes to Berlin on a week-long conference, where a senior German colleague takes her to Tempelhofer Park. In that large, flat plain, a former airport now given over to public recreational use, they walk purposelessly until they come to an area cordoned off by ropes with signs her friend translates for her: 'Skylarks breeding, please do not enter.' The area is flat, empty, covered with dense grass and other low vegetation that rise barely ten or twenty centimetres above the ground.

'Where are the skylarks?' she asks. A long poem from school-days tries to surface in her mind but the only words that emerge are 'unpremeditated art'.

'There, those things that are flying up from the grass, can you hear them?' her friend replies.

Those things? Does he mean the one or two little sparrow-like nothings, grey and negligible, that appear to be rising and falling above the grass?

'There,' he points, 'there, another one – do you see?'

'But . . . but . . . they're so tiny, you can hardly see them.'

'Can you hear them singing?'

This takes some time as she has to make a conscious effort to filter out all the ambient noise: the cheeping of birds, children playing in the distance, shreds of music, laughter, conversation, shouts, other sounds of clamorous human life.

'Let's lie down,' he suggests, 'and watch them rise up out of their nests.'

She still can't see them. The late afternoon sky is a huge orange bowl towards its rim, paling to a bluish white in the middle. She can see the specks of flying kites sent up by a group of people far away.

'There, look now, here, follow my finger,' he says urgently.

A tiny creature, hardly bigger than an infant's palm, flutters up, rising and rising.

'Listen! It's singing.'

The cheeping that she had been trying to tune out is the skylark's song. And now that she concentrates on it, it reveals itself as far from a generic background chirping of birds. It is a sustained flight of singing, note after note after note, strung out in a continuous curving, waving line, as if what's issuing from that tiny creature's mouth is an unbroken spool of colour. It remains audible, even if decreasingly so, as the bird ascends and becomes smaller even than a speck, almost disappearing into the light of the sky above and behind it. She is transfixed, by both the feat of the song and the ascent.

'The song advertises to the female his fitness as a mate,' he says. 'The longer he can hold the song and can stay aloft, the more attractive he becomes.'

She can't bring herself even to breathe. The bird is no longer discernible. If she were to turn her eyes away to a different spot in the sky, she knows that she wouldn't be able to see it if she looked back at the original point. Then suddenly, tumbling out of the air in a perfect straight line, the bird drops down to the ground and is lost in the green.

'He's exhausted himself in the display, our spunky hero. Oh look, here's another one.'

They lie there watching the birds and hearing their songs as they emerge, one at a time, giving marks out of ten, until the light fades and the blue of the sky darkens. The pause between the larks rising becomes longer and longer until the dark and the silence coincide and they get up to leave.

She walks back with her friend towards Neukölln, shielded in an armour of magic. Her life is changed.

V

It's difficult to sing a bird's song, or to mimic it so that it sounds even passably like the real thing, not just an imitation or a representation. Mimicry and mimesis are at variable distances from reality. The chief problem with perfect imitation of birdsong arises not for reasons to do with difficult music – after all, so much music that is atonal exists for the human voice – but for reasons of biology: human vocal cords were not meant to produce sounds that are indistinguishable from those of a piano, or a dolphin, or a cockatoo. Or, more precisely, humans *cannot* produce that kind of a sound – it is a matter of biological incapability; evolution saw no reason why humans should sound like chaffinches.

She knows, better than anyone, all of this.

She spends her spare time – what there is – learning to produce birdsong, a simple one like a little owl's, say (very difficult ones such as a blue tit's or a robin's will be forever beyond her), and although she fails and fails and fails, she is relentless in her trying. Like all beginnings, it's harmless, a melding of curiosity, passion, and the natural consequence of vocalizing an earworm. She listens to birdsong for eight to ten hours every day, every note broken down in a spectrographic analysis, and the larger units too, syllables and phrases. It's not a surprise, at first, to anyone that occasionally she should attempt to whistle a rendition, whistling being a tiny bit closer to the timbre and pitch and vibration of a bird's song than anything the human vocal range can produce. Then one day the humming begins. It's appropriately sotto voce to start with, then louder and louder, stuck in the same rut as a vinyl is when the stylus slips over a scratch, repetitive and atonal like birdsong is, sure enough, but, in the context of a lab filled with humans, embarrassing, first, then very quickly, alarming.

There are discussions among others how to stop it, a stuttering trickle of complaints. But the steady and reliable stream of groundbreaking publications coming out of the research from the lab means that a core of people choose to overlook the lab chief's idiosyncrasies as a minor irritant, something mildly entertaining. A junior scientist even engages with it, asking her to try out easier bird calls first before moving on to the far more difficult business of song. 'If you can get the pitch right in a luring or contact call,

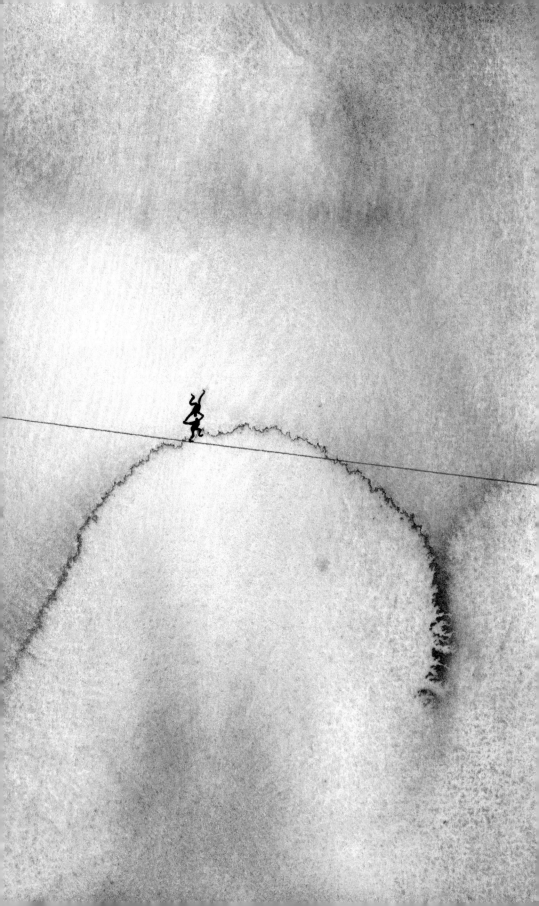

that alone would be terrific. The trills and buzzes in song are just soooo difficult!' he says.

And the publications make the small scientific community studying the auditory cortex, the neural coding of sounds, the neural substrates responsible for the learning of sounds, the question of whether these substrates are innate or learned, and a host of related and interlinked subjects sit up and take notice. There is a series of papers in the *Journal of Neurobiology, Nature, Journal of Comparative Neurology, Science, Annual Review of Neuroscience, Animal Behaviour, PNAS*, and others, and a number of them in edited collections (one of which, in a book bearing the title *Neural Mechanisms of Communication*, creates a big splash). Those who appreciate the painstaking, minutely-focused rigours of science, the exhaustive legwork, find revelatory the establishment of the neural hierarchy, particularly in subcortical structures, for learned vocal control in songbirds and the corresponding hierarchies in primates and humans. There is even a clever paper on how beak gape – the width of the opening of a bird's beak – is correlated to the pitch of the song. At a conference, she and two of her co-authors receive a long, sustained round of applause for their paper identifying 'a forebrain motor programming network for the learned song of zebra finches'. Scientific communities are not exactly known for their spontaneous emotional responses, so when another paper, 'Reafferent thalamo-"cortical" loops in the song system of oscine songbirds', despite its admission that the role of nucleus HVc in song production still remains unclear, receives another such ovation, a different kind of attention is focused on the work coming out of her lab.

But for her all this is a series of stepping-stones to where she really wants to go.

VI

A childhood fun lesson – watching birds land and perch on and take off from the huge tree outside their mother's window and learning their names – curdles into something else. When they were little, the children had watched with momentary wonder

these quick creatures flitting or preening or singing or shuttling along the branches, and had enjoyed their mother teaching them the names of the different species. Look at how big the magpie is compared with the robin, notice that it's black and white, has a large tail, look at the rust-coloured bib of the tiny robin... Now they are sat at the window and locked inside the room with specific instructions, which are incomprehensible to them: use a specific colour for each species and draw a series of dynamic pictures, unfolding in time, of their heterogeneous group distribution, then correlate these with their calls and songs. Look and hear. Eyes and ears. The only things that matter, eyes and ears.

The only things that have made her. Everything, she wanted to say, everything that has made her.

A father who owned a cornershop, a mother who stayed at home. A father whose mantra was, 'You have to be ten times better than the people in this country to get even a tenth of the attention and rewards they are given.' As if it weren't his country too; arrived from somewhere else, a somewhere else she had a very fuzzy notion of, but nevertheless more than half his life spent here, did that not make him part of the 'people of this country'? What an enormous distance her parents had come, a measure they kept crossing daily in what her father would keep referring to as 'this country' until the day he died.

And a mother who cowered from the alien world outside, all the light slowly extinguishing from her eyes, and all her energies poured into cooking and keeping her small family physically nourished and, she hoped, content; happiness did not come into it; what one had was happiness. She would have found the question, 'Are you happy?' incomprehensible, a kind of strange, riddle-like question conceived of and asked by the alien minds of 'this country'. It wasn't a question that would ever have occurred to people back home.

Back home. Of course.

Yet the distance their only daughter – impossibly bright and talented – opened up between her and them was far greater than the distances they had traversed to leave behind a place they called home. Always the 'first in class' in the fee-paying school her parents scrimped and saved and constrained their lives to send her to, she would come to see the turning point as a new urgency, a purposive matter, after thugs petrolbombed her father's cornershop and the police mysteriously couldn't catch anybody, citing a lack of clues and evidence and leads. For her, eight years old at the time, something changed in the nature of her consciousness of the two pairs of eyes boring into her all the time, willing her with every fibre of their beings to make something better, higher of her life. And she did. Her parents did not bully her, nag her, keep at her, but something in the mute, relentless steadiness of their longing for her to be ten times better, and the implied sense of all that her achievement would bring about, did its slow work inside her.

Nothing existed for her outside the poem she was reading, the partial differential equations in her problem set, the ordnance survey map she had been asked to read. The intensity was a force field around her – it held her peers, her teachers, her parents, everyone at bay. She didn't have friends; she didn't seem to need any. She held her tongue when the maths teacher was out of his depth, or the Eng Lit teacher didn't know where the volta came in a Shakespearean sonnet. She finished school and entered university at the age of fourteen. At twenty-one, she had a PhD in neuroscience. The world, as most people understood the term, in relation to the matrix of individual, social, even global and historical and political relationships they were embedded in, did not interest her. What she was searching for was an understanding of the deep structure of things, an answer to the biggest – and perhaps only – mystery in life, namely, the hinge between things which are distinct, separate yet inextricable, continuous, such as body and mind, sign and meaning, thought and dream . . .

There are days when her children are not fed. They go to school with crumpled, unwashed clothes, recycled days on end. The school writes to her that in one particular week the children have not been collected on three occasions after school. The letters remain unopened. The school calls her. She hears that her children have been caught stealing other students' lunches – can there be anything amiss at home? At the meeting with the school Principal, she plays a recording of a chaffinch song and says, 'Now, two things: first, pay careful attention to the pauses between each call,

and second, let's try to determine if the notes are exact repetitions or if there are some variations going on. OK, let's time the pause between each call.' It is after this meeting that the Principal gets in touch with the children's father.

She locks both children in the study upstairs one morning, sets up a laptop to play a three-minute recording of the song of the Eurasian great tit – *Parus major,* she parses, habitually – on a constant loop and asks them to master it. Simple enough: nine notes, no trills, no buzzes, pi-pi-pi-pi pi-pi-pi-pi-pi, rising and falling simply and alternately, although the pitch would be difficult to get right. Still, they are little, they can vocalize certain frequencies that would be beyond an adult. By lunchtime they have got the hang of only the number of notes and the basic rhythm; disappointing, although she knows the entire literature about sensitive periods for speech learning, even the distinction between limitation in learning to produce speech and limitation in perceptual learning. It is neurobiology 101. And it is the most basic kind of error, or madness, to imagine and instigate an inter-species vocal learning exercise (even she knows that it couldn't be dignified by the term 'experiment'). Still, she has her own reasons. These are stepping-stones to where she really wants to go.

The order of birdsong turns difficult. By the time she catches hold of them to put them on to the impossible and extraordinarily beautiful and long song of the song thrush – *Turdus philomelos,* she tells them, of the robin family – they start hiding from her. They have terror in their eyes, in the set of their mouths, when she herds them upstairs. The boy has begun to whimper. The girl is frozen. Halfway through the ten-minute segment of the song, both of them are whimpering. There is no daddy to save them at the end of the day because daddy is away on a business trip. She is never cruel, just focused, obsessive. She locks them in and says she will let them out at lunchtime. But she does not, because an idea has occurred to her – she wants to look at a set of 'barcodes' of neuron spikes in the auditory cortex of birds and for that she has to go to the lab. When she returns, around ten in the evening, the people from Social Services are at her doorstep.

And all through her days and nights, the intermittently bubbling stream, sometimes subterranean, sometimes on the surface, audible and visible, of an unanswered question: in that storybook, how did the man know how to read the private language of the dreams of the island-children? If he knew how to scramble their dreams so that no child knew which musical instrument embodied whose dream, then he surely must have known how to read them. Or could the scrambling have been a result of his *inability* to understand, something unintended but springing from an unsolvable constraint?

She spends hours standing at her window, or lying in bed when the will or the energy to get up and face her life is lacking, looking out at the forever-changing drama on the branches of the tree, until the dying of the light sends the birds home. Things have to turn extraordinarily complex before they can turn simple again. She has known this in her blood and nerves and bones from the very beginning of adult intellectual inquiry. Every scientist does. The world is simple to experience, difficult to understand in its details, workings, and effects. A machine is beautiful; the machinery, complex and head-spinning. Understanding involves formalization and any formal language is difficult and time-consuming to learn, master, and make malleable for your particular purposes. How simple, for example, a tree is, but the moment you begin to ask about its constituent elements, how it lives, nourishes itself, makes its own food, traps light, delivers nutrients from the roots to the tip, you have moved to indelible complexity. Who would have thought that a simple, magical thing such as the dawn chorus involved a hierarchy of information-processing in the avian auditory microcircuit? The deeper you delve, the more impossible it seems to reemerge to the surface – in other words, you are drowning – and experience anew the older, bigger picture, the earlier simplicity. And that is exactly what she wants to do.

Who knows when meaning becomes intent?

The first step towards where she wants to go lands her somewhere unexpected. At a game theory conference, she takes on signalling theory formalizations of bird call as evolutionarily stable strategies via a strange, unorthodox route. She maps the algebra of the signalling almost exactly on to the algebra of a two-party simple cheap talk game – so far, so predictable – and while her model obviously does not assume that birds consciously select their signal to maximize a payoff, she adds a strange spin to the assumption in biological models that the process of natural selection will lead to strategy profiles in which mutant behaviour has lower reproductive fitness than equilibrium behaviour. While running through the static and dynamic solution concepts similar to Nash Equilibrium and its refinements, she slips in – as if by chance, as if all her life she has not been preparing for this moment – the idea for a new definition of language. There are no questions, no comments – everyone is too puzzled and surprised by this turn of algebra towards a pop-version of philosophy and linguistics, even ethology, to formulate their thoughts. Everyone seems to be thinking, are we sure that she's claiming what we think she's claiming? But how can she? That's the domain of insanity.

At lunch-break, there's a considerable buffer of space between her and other participants. Eyes are quickly averted, people seem too intent on their conversations when she passes by. A wild-haired, scruffy man comes up to her while she's helping herself to salad and begins a conversation. Why is a theory of the mind of the human mind and human mind only. Isn't your starting point one of an acknowledgement of the ultimate frontier of its limitation, which is its absolute and fundamental inability to get into a non-human mind, even a bird's. And this despite all the technological advances, all the almost daily accumulation of news on the moving frontier: trees communicating via fungal networks, bees showing an ability to add and subtract, fish recognizing themselves in the mirror, cows differentiating between individuals of their own kind, Alston's singing mice taking turns to hold what can only be called a conversation ... What might the aggregation say. Maybe time for some humility now. The mathematization is

important, he says, I've posted some stuff online, including some proofs of a more formal nature on aspects of.

At the end of which she notices the wild, glittering eyes of the man, the gaze both too-focused and adrift, the foam-white of gathered spittle at the corners of his mouth, that same strenuous attempt on everyone's part to leave a decontamination zone around them. She thinks, Do I appear like him to the others here, and dabs the corners of her mouth with the scrunched-up paper napkin in her hand.

She publishes the paper in the most respected analytical philosophy journal. Within six months, it receives no less than eighty-four citations, of which just over three-quarters are from neuroscientists. They are almost all condemnatory, from both the philosophy side and the science.

A surprisingly less buttoned-up note of dissent is sounded at an interdisciplinary conference on the philosophy of language where linguists, philosophers, AI scholars, neuroscientists, psychologists, even economists, who of course have an answer, or at least an explanation, for everything, all come together in what is billed as the first multidisciplinary meeting of its kind on the one-problem-different-epistemologies model. She's wrestled with Frege and Wittgenstein and Quine and Tarski and Davidson for three years so that she cannot be accused of hubris or, worse, ignorance, yet she's unprepared for what happens. Using Davidson's radical interpretation theory as a lens on birdsong, her paper proposes dismantling the definition of language from its entirely human-languages-centred foundation to include birdsong and other animal communication codes. She brushes up very close to accusing almost all disciplines of speciesism in the way language has been defined so far in the history of human knowledge, and demolishes, or thinks she demolishes, every such criterion for the definitions: meaning, instrumentality, non-purposive communication, play, surplus, combinatorial plenitude, humour. Each domain is backed up with evidence. She cites the cases of isolate birdsong when the young birds have been separated from their parents, thus closing the opportunity for perceptual learning. People start rustling papers, coughing, whispering, even tittering; halfway through her presentation, some leave noisily while she's speaking. When she finishes, there's no applause. The silence weighs heavily in the air until it drops and shatters in the form of a lone laugh, derisory, mocking, incredulous. It breaks something other than the silence: someone stands up and says – Why are you here? You don't understand the very basic stuff of the philosophy of language. You're. Not. Even. Wrong.

A torrent bursts free. She alienates scientists by showing that she is bafflingly willing to engage with what they consider to be the unrigorous, lazy-thinking world of humanities; she has betrayed the superior world of science. And she infuriates humanists by exemplifying the typical arrogance of scientists, their long-held belief that scientists can go trampling in whatever field of knowledge they like, always assuming that they know better. She becomes redundant, almost forgotten, in the flinging of accusations and invectives across the boundary line between the two worlds. Mental states how can you ascribe. How can you a theory of truth. Humanities fascist. Scientific fundamentalist. Ignorant of mental content. Classic humanist woolly thinking, if thought it can be called. Algebra Kool-Aid victim. Hypermathematical patsy. Complex syntax what about the absence of complex syntax. A Velcro glove for the brain to take out all the wool. Soft in the head. Nominalist narrativist positivist obscurantist essentialist reductionist Davidsonian holistic terrorist blind

IX

The divorce had been quick. He hadn't bothered to claim his share of custody of the children, who had been one and three then. Looking back with disinterest on that chapter in her life, she feels as if the marriage had been a casual afterthought she and a slightly older graduate student had strayed into. She does not remember romance, nor courtship, passion, anything torrid, nor even the physicality necessary to have produced two children. Her abiding feeling of everything domestic is one of absentmindedness and, if she were given to thinking about what other humans felt or thought, she would have claimed that the same distraction was her ex-husband's default setting. It was possible to do the washing-up and be entirely engaged in a conversation or unknot a persistent mathematical problem inside your head or follow the counterpoint in a fugue; washing-up didn't require concentration and thought. In any case, those qualities of the mind and heart for her had long been given over, in their entirety, to another domain altogether, and now she's not only out of practice but, looking at his alien face in the family court – had she really lived with him all those years? – she considers the activity itself of bringing those kinds of attention to bear upon the ticking mechanism and the humdrum of everyday life to be antic, imaginary even.

In a strange mirroring of the divorce, she does not contest his suit for full custody of the children on grounds of endangerment, cruelty, neglect, children found locked in a room dehydrated hungry sitting in a pool of their excrement subjected to birdsong on endless unstoppable loop blah blah blah. How has she reached this point? Why is she here? she wants to ask, but only out of mild curiosity. She jots down an idea for pursuing a point about the elimination of spines in the LMAN of male zebra finches between 35 and 55 days.

She wants to ask a question of the children via their father via his lawyer – do the boy and the girl remember a book from their childhood about a stranger who shows up on an island of children and steals their dreams? – but the opportunity does not arise. There is a report from the Social Services at the hearing, maybe even a representative or someone who works for them.

Her only regret is that she hadn't caught the children at the stage of extreme learning plasticity, isolated them from all human sounds, and played them only one particular birdsong while they were held in captivity for the entirety of the critical period. Maybe two years or three? Such regret. Lost opportunity. The impossibility of rewinding history and letting it spool out again in a different direction. All that time and energy wasted in bringing them into the world, in looking after them. All her thoughts. Such regret.

Now, such anger.

X

Again in winter. There's a green-bibbed great tit, the black dome of its head swivelling from one side to the other as if ferociously impatient with whatever it sees. Then a call – 8-9, in dotted pairs, pi-pi | pi-pi | pi-pi | pi-pi pause pi-pi | pi-pi | pi-pi | pi-pi-pi. Repeated and repeated and repeated. Alone on the great tree, a first note on a stave in a virgin composition book. Two other tits fly in and perch on a slightly higher branch. One male, one female. The singing tit continues as if it hasn't seen the new arrivals, then stops. Silence. All three seem to be looking at everything else but each other. The first singing tit begins again, but the notes have changed and are clustered slightly differently now; no longer 8-9, but 9-10, again in pairs. Three more fly in but sit dispersed in the branches. If they're all listening to the song, there seems to be no visible sign. In fact, if anything, they seem to her human eye to be paying attention to other things. A quick quiver of green and black and white and grey, and one of them flies to sit on a branch where two more are sitting. Then, without any warning, all of them take off. A brief audible whirr of air as they fly up. Silence and emptiness. A huge hulking jackdaw on a top branch, peering down with great intent. First one, then two dancing magpies on the ledge of the roof terrace. Slip in between the railings on to the terrace, out of her sight. No call, no sound. Oh look a robin clinging vertically on to the boiler vent in the wall, pretending to be a woodpecker. It flies out of sight after it notices her. Then four robins on the tree, all of them on the same branch. A call. Another chirrup. But no song. They fluff and preen, peck their own breasts, look up and sideways. Then one of them begins his trilling, warbling, seemingly aleatory song. She can see his beak gape. A plane passes overhead. The song continues unabated. It thrills through the body of the bird. She can see that the creature is rocked by the energy that has gone to produce the song. Again, the other robins seem more interested in other things. How can it be that there aren't neuron spikes going off in their brains? On an unknown signal, they fly away, leaving the singing robin alone, pouring his heart out. Her own is thumping. Directed or undirected song? He stops, darts his head this way and that, looks into the distance for one two three four five seconds, then flies off too. Silence. Just when she was beginning to. A clattering of pigeons. Not interesting. The tits are back – pigeons and tits all together now on the tree. How unmindful of each other, almost with intent, you'd think. The pigeons are positively lumbering in their sideways shuffle along the branch compared with the electric darts and shivers of the smaller birds. Nothing, just silence. The only sound the roar in her ears of her own blood. The cawing of a crow from somewhere out of the field of her vision. A magpie cries. Then magic enters her life again: a flock of glossy starlings – not quite a murmuration but a chattering, certainly – descends on to the branches, dozens and dozens of them, their sociable, unceasing talk so varied, so wide-spectrum that the chorus brings her to the destructive edge of elation. Chirps, coos, squeaks, pips, whistles, clicks, chatter, tiny musical phrases, a parabola of a call starting up swinging down then going up again, squawks, clicking that resembles swift percussion, cheeps oh dear god. The tree is restless with the life of sound. What are they hearing? What are they talking about? Twee-twee-twee-pip. Wheeeeee. Chip-chip-chip-chip-creeeee. That parabola again and again flinging itself in, drawing itself back. Her eyes and ears are letting the torrent of the whole wide world in. The bigger picture. Even without looking she can see – and hear – a pair of blackbirds fossicking around in the dried leaves in the garden four floors below. Will they join? She can no longer hear the pumping of her blood in her head. The male blackbird begins the long run of a phrase, the light changes dramatically as if a screen or filter has been removed by off-stage technicians, and in the flood of everything she knows she understands all. She understands the conversation that is happening, first picking out the phrases and sentences and half-sentences in the madness of the starlings, much as one can identify snatches of talk here and there in a restaurant loud with commingled human conversations, then the cleaner, sparer musical line of the blackbird's song running underneath that multitude of sound – she understands it all. They are talking. They are talking to each other, and they are talking to each other across species, and she can hear it all. She is levitating. She has stepped back to the bigger picture and she can see everything connecting. She opens the lower sash of the window with utmost care to avoid disturbing the birds outside. Here is everything and she can understand.

The children come to see her in hospital. She cannot be left unsupervised; there is a white-uniformed attendant in the room. She doesn't recognize them for the first few seconds; they look a little changed, they have grown, they are different people from who they were when she saw them last. There is a hollow feeling in her, as if she's falling from a huge height. The children are formal, polite, diffident, even a little...cowering, is that it? A little bit wary, as a child would be with a stranger who approached it in the street? Is the attendant in the room worried about her safety or the children's?

The boy is holding a book. He offers it to her. She doesn't understand if it's a gift or...or something else, such as a silent request to be read to, much as he made when he was younger. A different country altogether. She tries to imagine what was going through his head – did he think it was going to soothe her, bring her back? If so, was it a hope? That falling, hollowing feeling again.

She asks them if they remember a book from their childhood, perhaps even one which she had read out to them at bathtime or bedtime, a story about a stranger stealing children's dreams and fashioning musical instruments out of them, so that he could sell them back to the children...

They both shake their heads, silently.

The book she accepts from the boy is not a picture book in which the words are few and the art predominant, instead something for slightly older children, still illustrated, but with an increasing density of writing that demotes the pictures to a fewer-and-further-between status. A collection of original fairy tales from different parts of the world, she reads. A story about the spirits of tigers haunting children in the villages around the mangrove deltas of the Bay of Bengal. A story from Russia featuring a witch's house with chickens' feet that can move and relocate itself and spin around. From Mexico, a girl whose copious tears on hitting the ground grow into trees, resulting in a dense forest that ultimately immures her.

Then a story that begins with a full-page illustration: seen from the upper branches of birch trees – the white bark on all of them is a beautiful and visually startling touch – on which several birds are perched, it shows a boy and a girl, hand in hand, on the forest floor far below, looking up at the birds, each of which has a few short wavy lines of unreadable runic script coming out of its open beak. Her hands shake as she turns the page to the words.

She skim-reads to get from beginning to end as quickly as possible. It's the story of a brother and sister, Ludovic and Lyudmilla, who have escaped to a birch forest after seeing their village, and everyone they know in it, destroyed in a fire. The trees are full of birds, the forest thrumming with song and chatter and flutter. Suddenly the siblings realize that they can understand what the birds are saying.

The hollow feeling has changed to a fine, focused tension.

The visiting children are still with expectation.

Ludovic tells Lyudmilla what he has heard. Lyudmilla tells him that she has heard something entirely different. They try to establish if both are hearing the same song, and when they do, they find that the same sound holds wildly different meanings for each of them.

She cannot read further. Against all the force of her will, something makes her turn the page. It's an illustration double-spread: the boy and the girl are looking at each other, baffled, sad, imprisoned in their Babels. Up above, the runes continue to pour from the birds' mouths in a festive confetti.

Cambridge, Massachusetts

COLOPHON

THE CAHIERS SERIES · NUMBER 34
ISBN: 978-1-909631-33-5

Series Editor: Dan Gunn
Associate Series Editor: Daniel Medin
Design: SYLPH EDITIONS DESIGN
Set in Giovanni Mardersteig's Monotype Dante

With thanks to the San Francisco Foundation
for its generous support.

CENTER FOR WRITERS & TRANSLATORS
THE AMERICAN UNIVERSITY OF PARIS

SYLPH EDITIONS, LONDON | 2020

THE AMERICAN
UNIVERSITY 55
of PARIS YEARS

center for writers and translators

SYLPH
EDITIONS

www.sylpheditions.com · www.aup.edu